For anyone who feels unnoticed

Henry Holt and Company, LLC
Publishers since 1866
175 Fifth Avenue
New York, New York 10010
mackids.com

Library of Congress Cataloging-in-Publication Data is available
LCCN: 2014009173
ISBN 978-0-8050-9825-9

Henry Holt books may be purchased for business or promotional use. For information
on bulk purchases, please contact the Macmillan Corporate and Premium Sales Department
at (800) 221-7945 x5442 or by e-mail at specialmarkets@macmillan.com.

First Edition—2014
Printed in the United States of America by Phoenix Color, Hagerstown, Maryland

3   5   7   9   10   8   6   4   2

Little Elliot

BIG CITY

Story and pictures by Mike Curato

Henry Holt and Company New York

*L*ittle Elliot was an elephant.

He was different
in many ways.

Little Elliot loved living in a big city, but sometimes it was hard being so small in such a huge place.

He had to be careful not
to be stepped on.

He had trouble opening doors.

And he could never catch a cab.

Even life at home was a bit challenging.

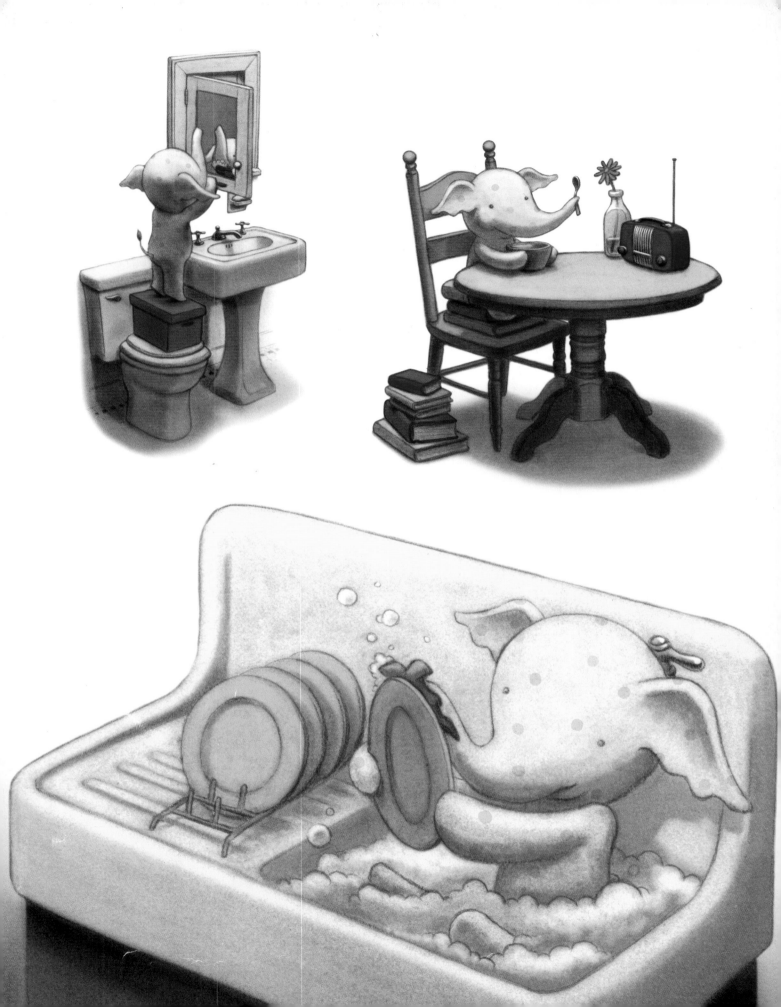

Still, Elliot enjoyed
the little things . . .

. . . small treasures . . .

. . . and most of all, cupcakes!

One day, Elliot tried to
buy a cupcake, but no
one noticed him.

Walking home, Elliot was so sad that
he barely noticed a thing . . .

. . . until he saw someone even littler than himself,
who had an even bigger problem.

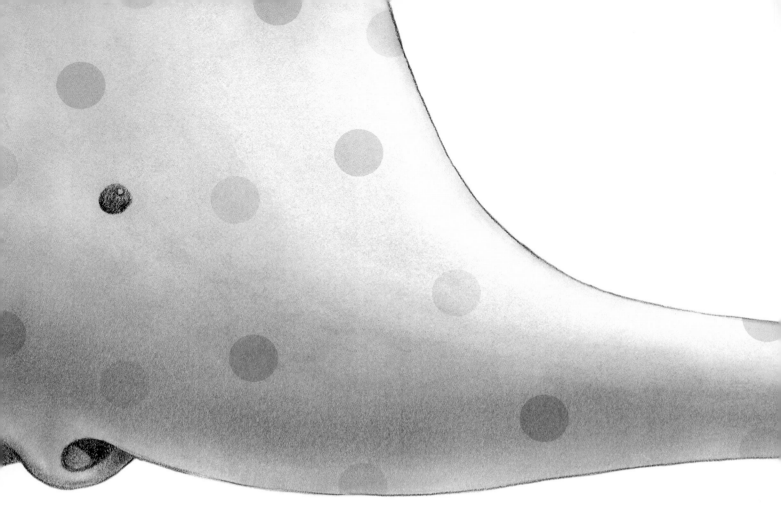

"Hello, Mouse. What is wrong?" asked Elliot.

"I'm trying to reach some food
but I'm too small," said Mouse.
"And I'm so very hungry."

"I can help!" said Elliot.

Elliot felt like the tallest elephant in the world!

The next day, Mouse came
with Elliot to the bakery.

Elliot finally
got his cupcake!

. . . and something even better.